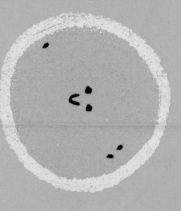

A kiss, a hug, and much
love to my boys:
Tim, Josh, and Nathan
—Dianne White

For Elizabeth & Henry—
my two favorite people
—Daniel Wiseman

hmhco.com

The illustrations in this book were produced digitally.
The text was set in Plumbsky Fat.

Library of Congress Cataloging-in-Publication Data is on file.

ISBN: 978-0-544-79875-5

Manufactured in China
SCP 10 9 8 7 6 5 4 3 2 1
4500700808

Goodbye
Brings
Hello

By Dianne White

Pictures by Daniel Wiseman

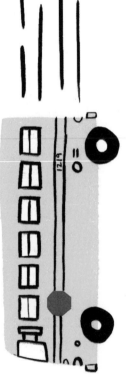

Houghton Mifflin Harcourt
Boston New York

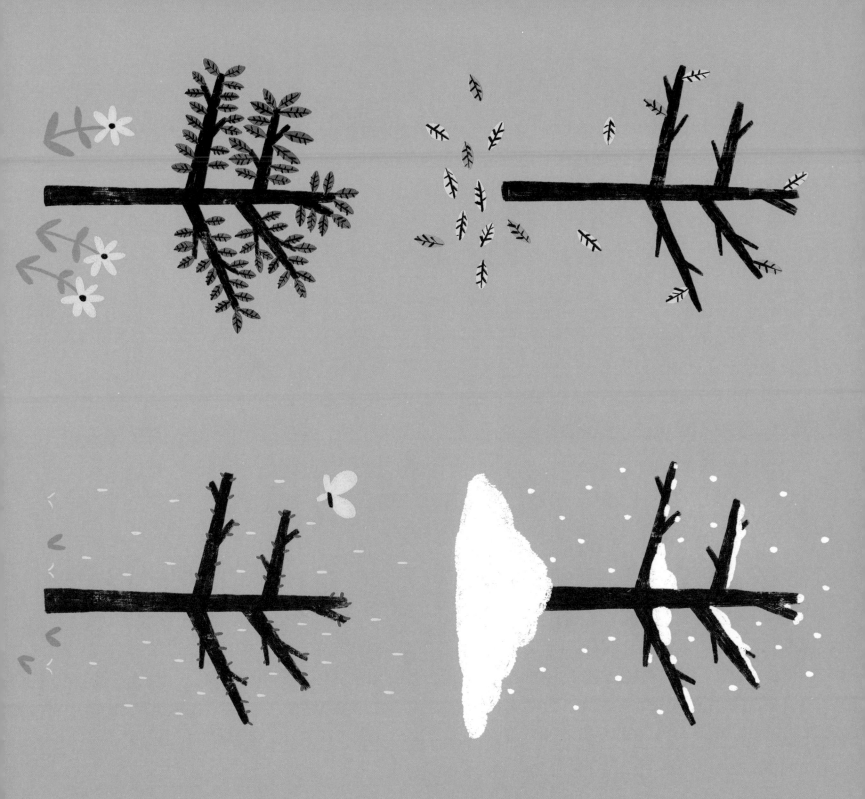

There are many ways of letting go.
With each goodbye, a new hello.

Feet fly up. Legs swing high.
Push Earth away. Hello, blue sky!

Last year's favorite,
Now too tight.

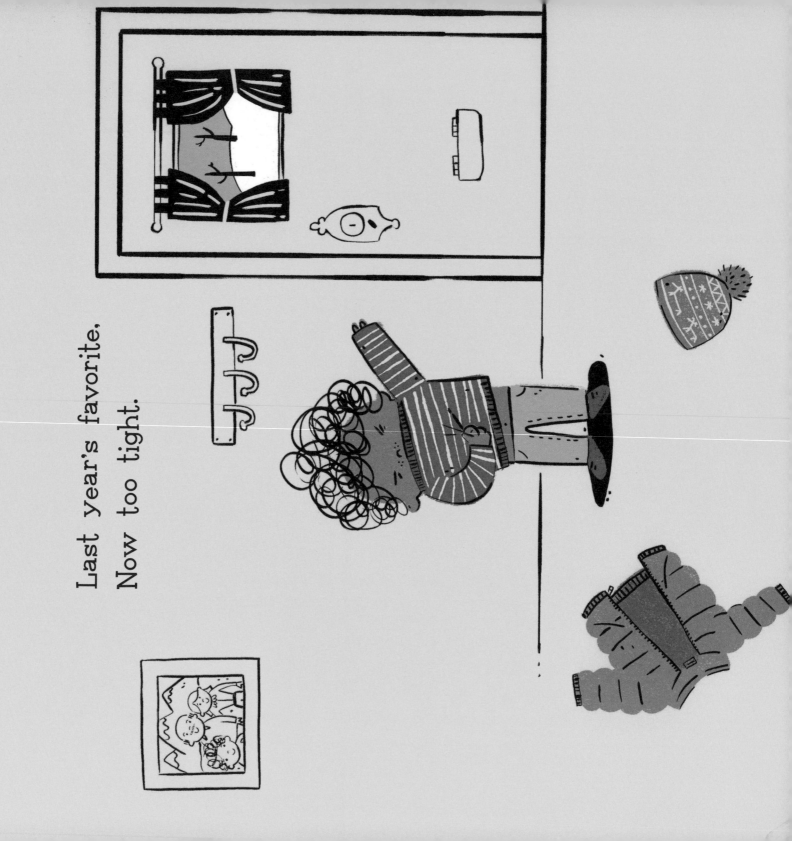

Button. Zip.
Fits just right.

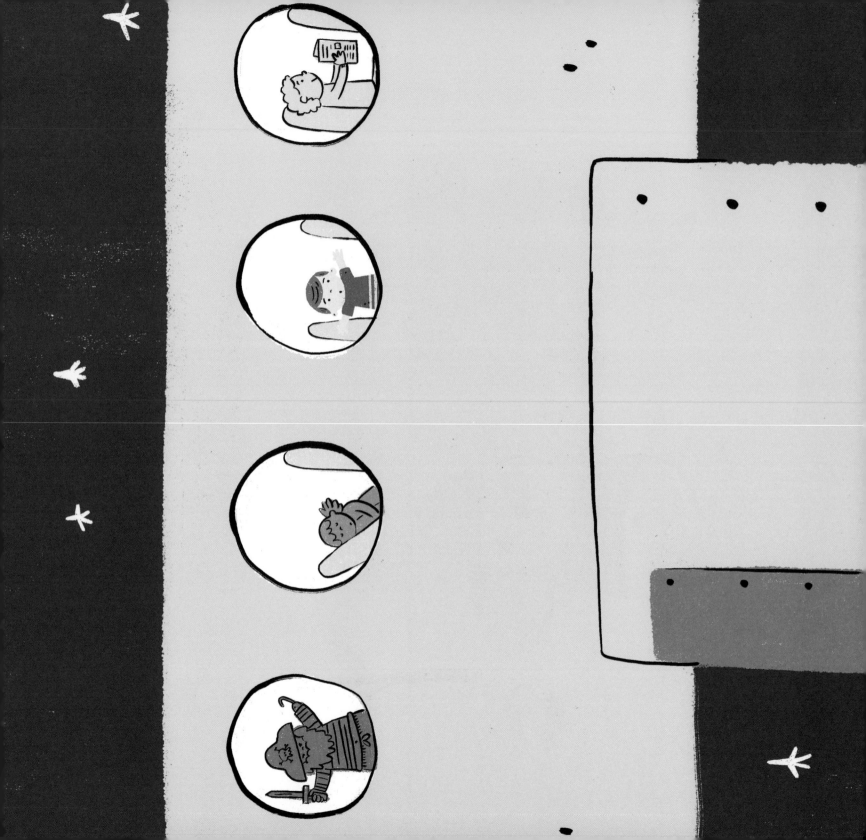

Leaving home.
Flying late.

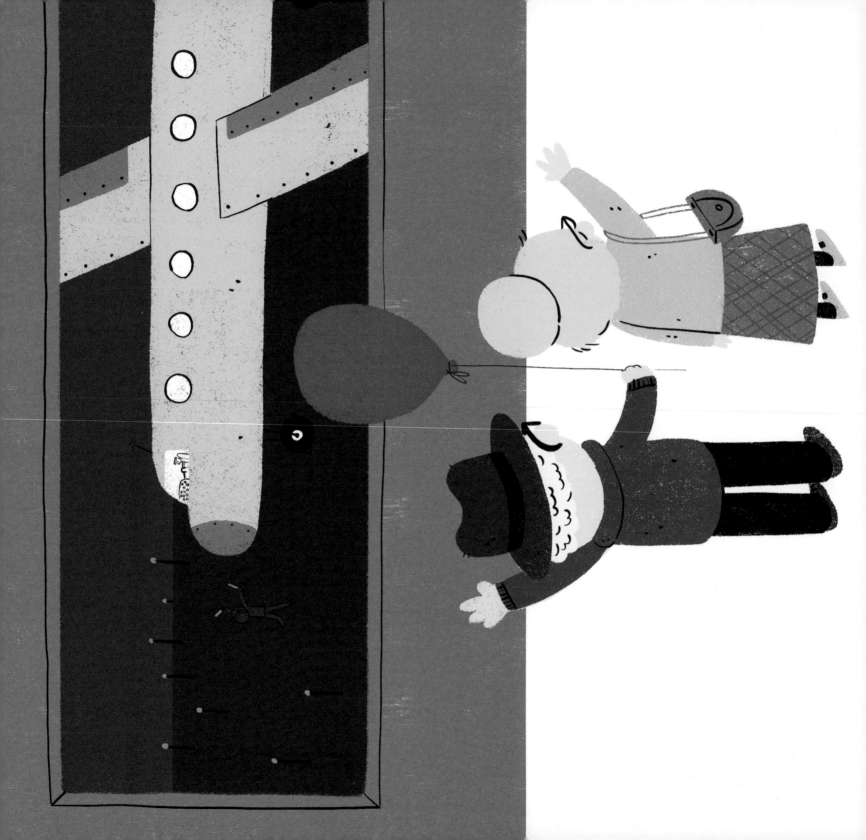

Look who's waiting
past the gate!

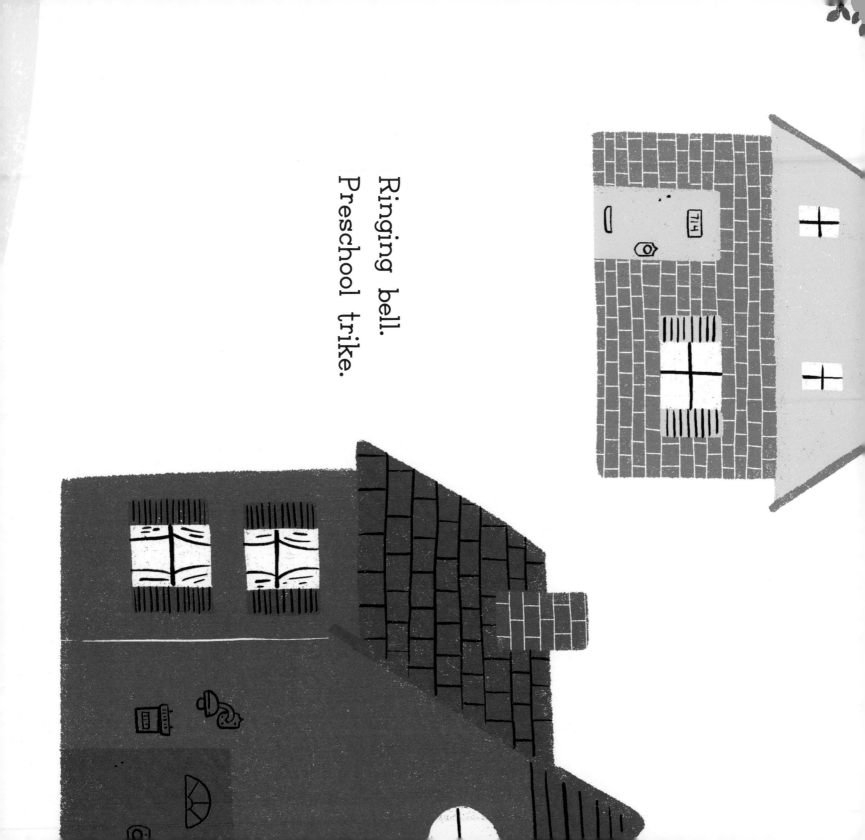

Ringing bell.
Preschool trike.

Wind in your face.
Big-kid bike.

On the edge.

One .... Two .....

5 FT

THREE!

Splash and paddle,
wild and free.

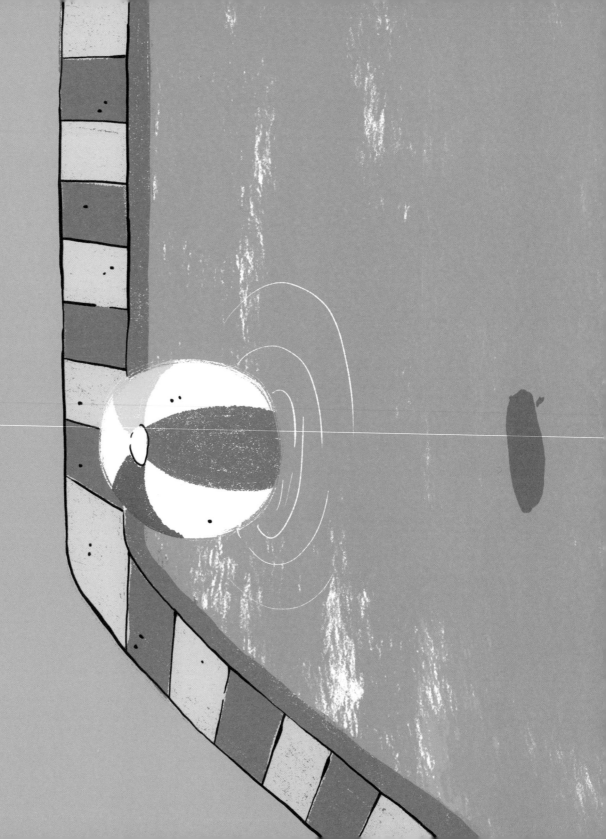

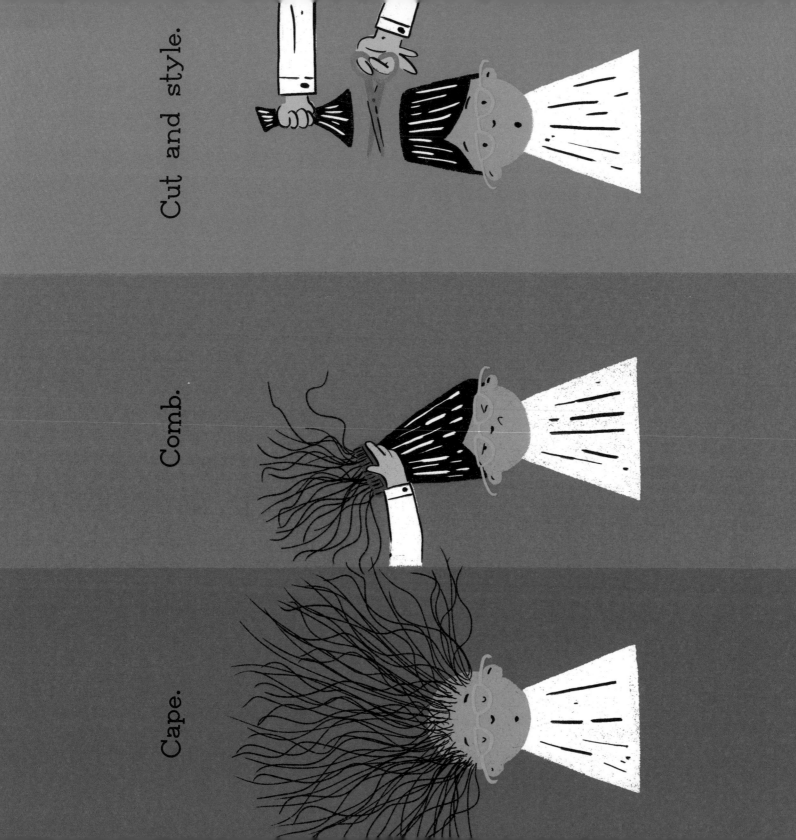

Cape.

Comb.

Cut and style.

Goodbye, frown.
Hello, smile.

Loop the laces.
Knot the bows.

So long,
Velcro-covered toes.

Chunky crayons.
Big designs.

Hello, letters on the lines.

Purple jelly.
Slice of bread.
By yourself.
Spoon and spread.

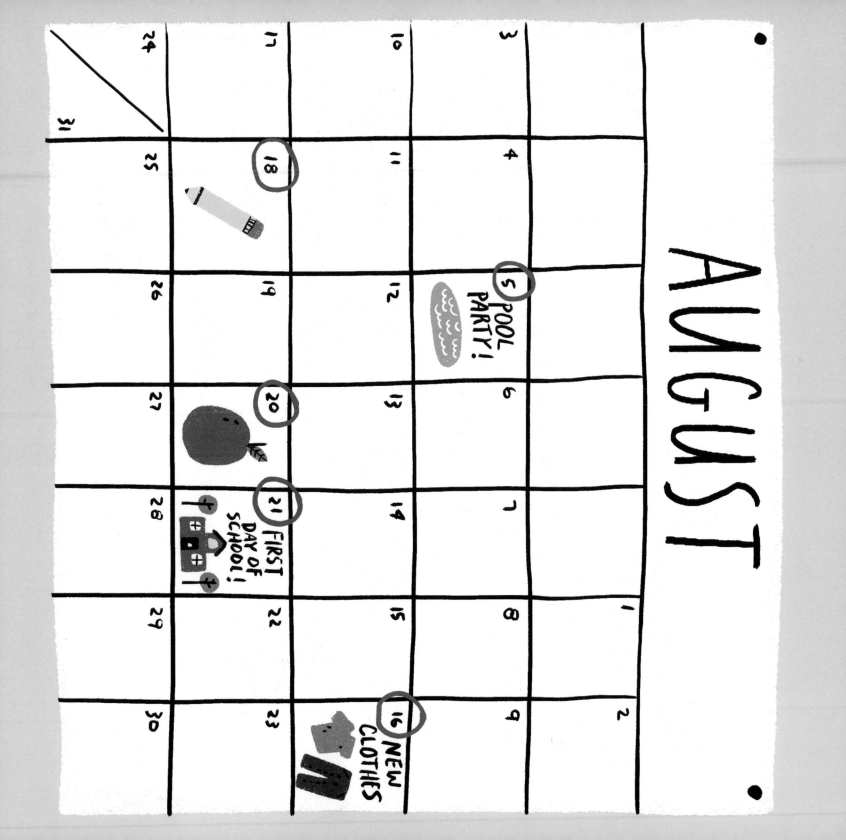

Snuggle Teddy. On your way.
Perhaps you'll make a friend today.

The world awaits. Will you explore?
Grab your pack. Open the door.

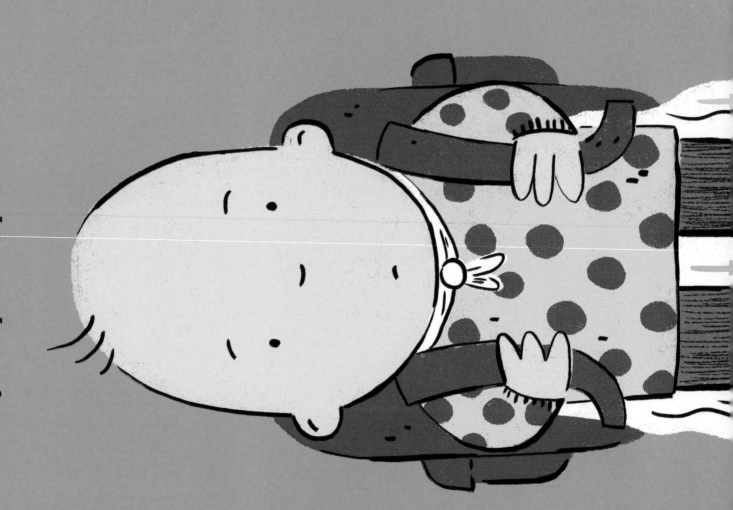

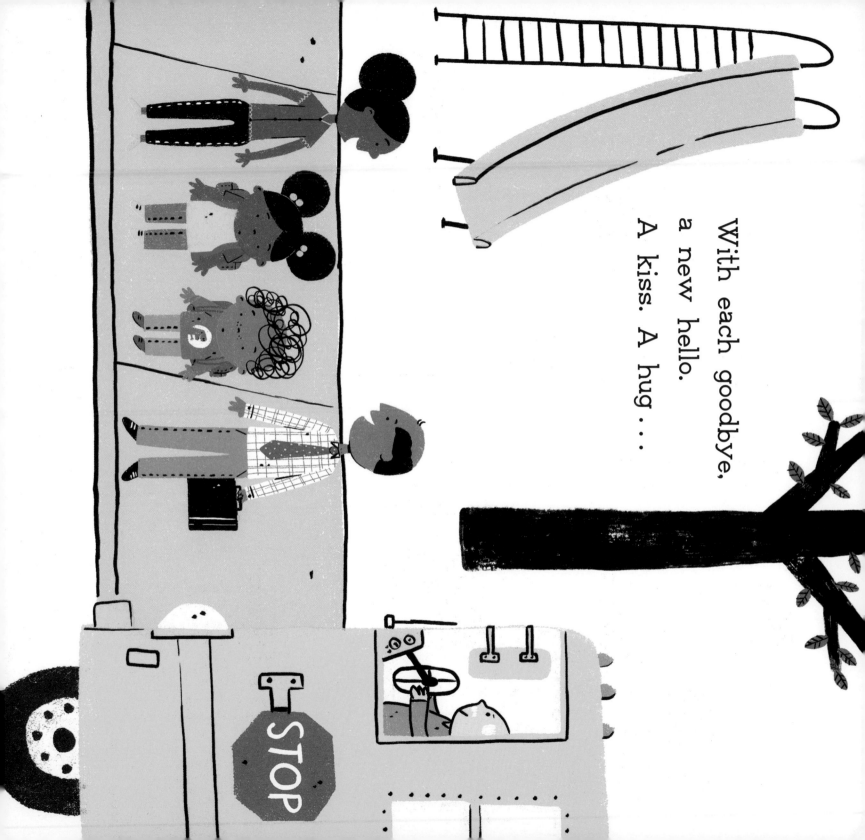

With each goodbye,
a new hello.
A kiss. A hug . . .

And off you GO!

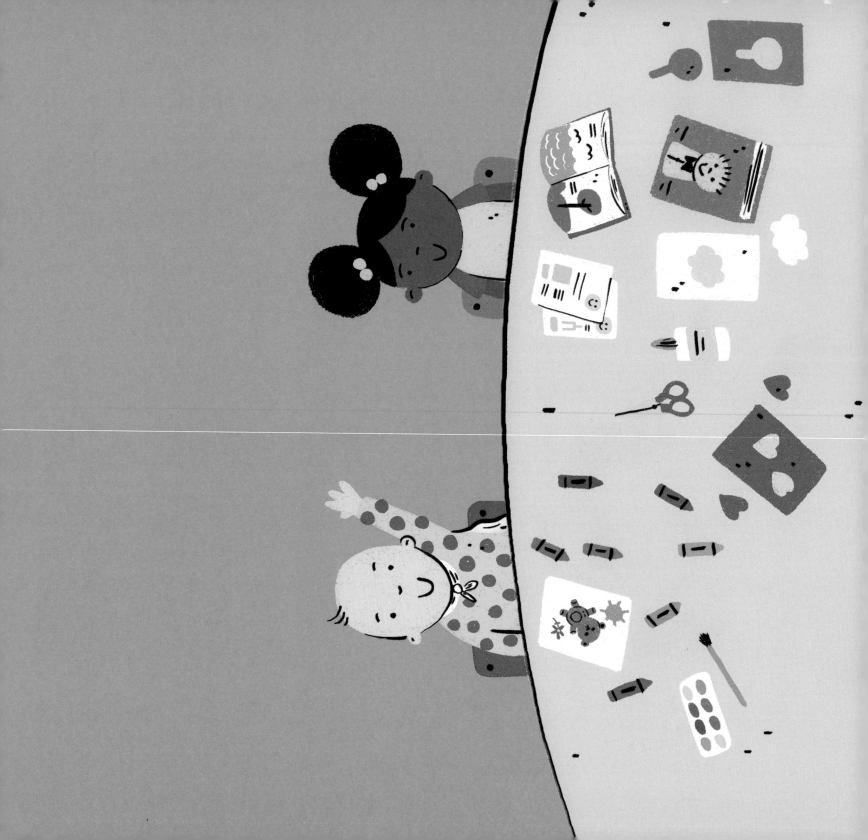